Contents

First published 2013 by Brown Watson
The Old Mill, 76 Fleckney Road
Kibworth Beauchamp
Leicestershire LE8 0HG

ISBN: 978-0-7097-2136-9
© 2013 Brown Watson, England
Printed in Malaysia

5 Minute Stories for Boys

Brown Watson

ENGLAND LE8 0HG

Treasure Hunt

Andy and Molly are excited. They are playing at pirates on board an old ship that is moored in the village harbour. The two of them run up and down, investigating all the old things on deck.

"Look, Andy – a treasure chest!" shouts Molly. "I wonder what's in it?"

When Molly tries to open the chest, she finds that it is locked. "Ooh, there must be something very special inside. Come and help me find the key!"

Their parents smile and watch the two pirates running around on deck. They know what the treasure is, because they put it there earlier.

Andy starts his search by looking in an old cannon. "It's really heavy," he says. "I can't move it at all. And my arms aren't long enough to reach inside."

Molly brings her torch and shines it down the barrel of the cannon. They can see that there is nothing in there, just a pile of leaves and twigs. "I think it is a mouse's nest," says Andy. "Hee hee, pirate mice!"

The children keep searching around on deck. Andy wants to lie in the hammock, but Molly won't let him. "We have to keep looking!" she says, and grabs his hand.

The kitchen on a ship is called the galley, and that is where the children decide to look next.

"Pirates ate maggoty biscuits and other horrible food," says Andy. "I don't think I'd like that part of being a pirate."

Molly is looking in an old barrel. She asks Andy to pass her the torch.
"Ooh," she giggles, and her voice sounds all muffled.
"More mice!
But definitely no key.
Where shall we look next?"

Andy has to pull Molly's legs to help her out of the barrel.
She nearly got stuck inside!

Molly and Andy are feeling brave now and decide to explore below deck. It is very dark down there. "What did pirates keep here?" whispers Andy.

"Prisoners!" teases Molly. "And guess what – more mice!"

They shine their torch around and look in all the hiding places, but still can't find a key. They are starting to get bored of this treasure hunt now. "And I'm getting hungry," says Molly.

Andy agrees, and they both laugh when his tummy rumbles and echoes around the dark room they are in. The dust is making them sneeze, so they climb back up the ladder and blink in the bright sunshine.

Molly wanders across the deck, kicking at
the sacks and sails that are scattered around.
Then she hears a metallic tinkle. She lifts the corner
of a sail, and sees gold glinting in the sun.
"Treasure!" she yells, and picks up a pile of gold coins.

She runs across to Andy who is also excited at
something he has found under a coil of rope.
The key to the chest!

The pair rush to unlock the chest and find
the treasure. "Yummy!" they shout, when
they find a perfect pirate picnic.
"This is our favourite thing of all!"

Hide and Squeak

Everyone knows that toys love to play. They love to play with their children, and they love to play on their own. Playing is what toys do best.

Tommy's toys play chase in the toy room. They have races to see who is the fastest. They try to beat each other at musical statues. Their favourite game of all is hide and seek.

Sidney the toy
snake and Jumbo
the toy elephant are
best friends. They like to
join in the games, but they
aren't always very good.

Jumbo is too big to hide very easily, and too slow
to win any races. Sidney always wiggles during
musical statues, and his squeak gives him away
in his hiding places.

Today, the two friends have decided to make up their own game. Jumbo blows up a balloon and then lets it go. The balloon flies around the room making a funny squealing noise. No one can guess where it will land!

Sidney wants to try the game next. He puffs and puffs into the balloon until it is big and round like the sun. Then he lets go and watches it zigzag to the ceiling and towards the four walls.

"EEEEEEEEEE-EEEEEEEEEE-EEEEEEEEEEE!" says the balloon, and all the toys in the toy room laugh.

Sidney blows up the balloon again. "EEEEEEEEEE-EEEEEEEEEE-EEEEEEEEEEE!" it goes, as it flies up into the air. The toys all think it is hilarious.

Something odd has happened to Sidney. When the others all laugh, he tries to join in, but no sound comes out. Sidney has lost his squeak!

Jumbo gives Sidney a big hug. "Don't worry," he says. "We'll help you find your squeak. I think perhaps it came out when you blew up that balloon! It did make a very good squeaking noise as it flew around the room."

Sidney is very scared. His Uncle Vernon lost his squeak, a long time ago, and he had to go to hospital. Sidney doesn't want to go to hospital!

Poor Sidney! The other toys feel very sorry for him. They all start to look for his squeak. Surely it must be somewhere in the toy room?

Jack looks to see if the squeak is in his box, but there is only his spring inside. Kitty Cat climbs up the curtains to check all the high places. Dooby Duck quacks excitedly when she hears a squeaking noise in the watering can, but then she finds that it is Mister Mouse. He has crawled right inside to see if Sidney's squeak is in there.

"Hmm," says Jumbo from inside the plants. "I bet we'll find it in this jungle. There could be all sorts of unknown things in here!"

Sure enough, Jumbo spies a bright yellow object deep in the undergrowth. He pokes around with his trunk until he can get it. "Look, Sidney – the yellow balloon! It might have your squeak inside it."

Sidney breathes a sigh of relief. Perhaps he won't have to go to hospital after all. As he sighs, a small squeak comes out. "Eeeeeee," sighs Sidney.

Jumbo turns to look at him. "Do that again," he says.

"Eeeeeeee…EEEEE…EEEEEEEEEEEEEEEEEE!" Sidney wiggles with delight.

"I know what happened," says Jumbo. "Your voice was playing hide and squeak!"

"Yes," says Kitty Cat. "And it's actually a lot better at it on its own!"

All of the toys roll around laughing. Thank goodness Sidney's squeak has been found.

Three Cheers for Danny

"Hurraaaaaaaaay!" cheered the crowds as Danny the dirt bike hurtled across the finish line in first place.

Danny loved to race, and he loved it even more when he won. Nothing could beat the roar of the crowds and the feel of zooming round and round the track at top speed. Danny lived for the smell and even the taste of the dirt and dust that kicked up all around him when he scrambled over the rough terrain of the racecourse.

He skidded to a halt beyond the finish line, kicking up even more clouds of dirt and dust.

"Well done, Danny," said his rider.
"Another trophy to add to our collection!"

As Danny drove back to the truck that would carry him home, his engine coughed and spluttered. He jerked and juddered slightly but then began to run smoothly once more.

Over the next few races, Danny found it harder and harder to keep up with the others. Every time he tried to increase his speed to pull himself through a corner, his engine stuttered. When he wanted to pile on the power for a long straight run at the finish line, he just didn't have the extra oomph he was used to. His pistons felt poorly, his cylinders were sick, and his exhaust was – well, exhausted.

Danny's rider pushed him onto the back of the truck and patted his handlebars. "I think we need to get you looked at," he said sadly.

A mechanic came to Danny's garage to give him a check-up. He took out his toolbox and rolled up his sleeves.

Poor Danny feared the worst – and he was right. "I'm afraid your racing days are over," said the mechanic. "You have taken in too much dust and dirt, and it's too dangerous for you to compete any more."

The mechanic could tell how sad this news was for Danny. He knew that Danny just adored racing round and round, and hearing the cheers of the people watching.

As he packed away his toolkit, the mechanic had an idea. "Do you like children?" he asked.

Danny wasn't sure. He had only ever been ridden by adults, and when he was racing he was going too fast to tell if his fans were young or old.

The mechanic brought his children and their friends to look at Danny. They gasped when they saw his huge engine and rough tyres. But they thought he was far too dirty to ride on. The mechanic cleaned him up, and then the children loved him. They climbed on his back and poked their fingers in his spokes.

Danny stood there patiently, but the mechanic could tell he was sad. "Am I going to spend the rest of my life here in this room?" Danny asked.
"I miss the zooming and the cheering."

The mechanic led Danny back to the truck and loaded him on the back.

"This is it," thought Danny. "Next stop – the scrapyard." A single drop of engine oil slid down his cheek.

Instead of driving to the scrapyard, the mechanic took Danny to the local fairground. Danny could see the roller coaster cars whipping up and down their track. "That looks like fun!" he thought. Then he saw the big wheel carriages going round and round. "I could cope with that!" he thought.

The mechanic had a better plan for Danny, though. He wheeled him across the grass to a merry go round and bolted him securely into place on its base.

A queue of children were waiting to go on the merry go round. Each of them wanted to ride on Danny's back. They laughed and yelled as they fought over who should sit on him first.

The ride operator pressed the start button and Danny moved round and round with the ride. Gradually, he got faster and faster. The children roared and threw their hands in the air. "Hurraaaaaaaaay!" they cheered as they flashed past their parents waiting at the side.

"Whee!" roared Danny. "This is fast fairground fun! Let's do it again and again!"

A Sticky Situation

It is the day of the village fair, and everyone has gathered together to have fun. There are rides to go on, games to play, and lots and lots of yummy food to try.

Fred the fire engine is on display. He is surrounded by children who want to climb inside and ring his bell. They put lots of sticky fingerprints all over him, but Fred doesn't mind.

"Can I sound the siren?" asks one little boy.
"Can I squirt the hose?" asks his sister.
"How fast can you go?" asks a boy
wearing a baseball cap.
"What's it like to rescue someone from a real
fire?" asks a girl with ribbons in her hair.

Fred smiles and lets Fireman Bob
do the talking.

The crowds grow bigger and Fireman Bob laughs at all the questions he is being asked. "This is hard work," he exclaims, wiping sweat from his face with a handkerchief. Then his walkie talkie springs to life.

"Quick, Fred!" shouts Fireman Bob. "We have a call out! Switch on your siren and let's get out of here!"

The crowds stand back and fire engine Fred drives carefully past them. "NEENAW NEENAW!" screams his siren as he hits the open road and speeds off. "Where to, Bob?"

Fireman Bob checks his instructions and steers Fred in the right direction. "We need to help Mrs Jennings on Penny Lane. There is lots of black smoke coming from her house. As fast as you can, please, Fred!"

Fire Engine Fred screeches into Penny Lane and stops smartly outside Mrs Jennings' house. There are clouds of black smoke billowing everywhere.

Fireman Bob leaps into action. He is a very good fireman. His team gets out the ladders and hoses while Bob rushes to check who is inside the house.

It is all very dramatic and exciting. Bob finds Mrs Jennings in the kitchen and hoists her onto his shoulder. He runs out of the house and carries her a safe distance away.

"Whatever are you doing?" she exclaims.

Bob and his team look puzzled. They are used to people saying thank you for being rescued! They quickly turn off the hoses and stop squirting water everywhere.

Mrs Jennings explains. "I was warming up my oven to bake some cakes, and then I smelt burning. When I opened the oven door, black smoke poured out. I think it must have been some spilled cake mix from the last time I was baking!"

The Firemen go back into the house to rescue the furniture they squirted with their hoses. Fortunately, the cake was in a tin, so that stayed dry! Mrs Jennings offers them all a slice before they head back to the fire station.

It feels calm and quiet in the station. Fire Engine Fred has had an unusual day. First, all of those children climbing all over him, and then the excitement of the smoking house!

Fireman Bob appears with two buckets of warm, soapy water. "How do you fancy a scrub, and then a rest?" he says to Fred, and starts to rub bubbles over Fred's sides. "Ooh, that tickles!" laughs Fred, and lets out a little whoop from his siren.

"Sorry, Fred," smiles Bob. "But you're covered in sticky food! I can see strawberry ice cream, candyfloss, and popcorn…and I do believe that's chocolate icing just there on the steering wheel! I can't imagine how that got there!"

Bob pats the fire engine dry and then turns out the lights. It might be another busy, sticky, smoky day tomorrow!

Slow Down Sonny

Farmer Riley lived on a busy but peaceful farm. His trusty tractor, Tony, helped him every day. Together, they fed and cared for the sheep, and kept the farm in good shape. They mended gates, put up fences, and made sure the animals had all they needed.

Tony and Farmer Riley didn't talk much, but they got along well. Tony was slow but steady, and he chugged along quietly to get the jobs done. He was happy working on the farm with Farmer Riley and the sheep.

One day, Tony heard a loud revving sound and the screeching of tyres. He looked up to the brow of the hill, by the farm entrance. There was a large cloud of smoke and dust moving down the track towards them.

Tony watched in astonishment as a bright yellow sports car hurtled into the farmyard and skidded to a halt. "Hi," said the car, "I'm Sonny. Pleased to meet you. What's your name?"

But before Tony could reply, the crazy car had zoomed full circle and accelerated into the distance.

As Tony pondered over what had just happened,
Farmer Riley came into the yard.

"Why d'you look so sad, Tony?"
asked Farmer Riley. "I hope it's nothing to do with
that new sports car. He's all revs and no
substance, you mark my words!"

Tony wasn't convinced. He couldn't stop thinking
about the sports car's sleek shape and skinny tyres.
He could still hear the meaty roar of the
engine in the distance.
If only he could drive so fast!

Farmer Riley patted Tony's huge tyre
and climbed into the driver's seat.
"Right, old chap," he said.
"There's lots to do today. First of all,
feeding. Then we need to sort
out some sheep for shearing.
Off to the top field and we'll
get this job done."

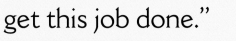

Tony trundled up the hill to the top field. The sheep were so used to Tony that they carried on grazing contentedly.

Sonny saw the farmer and his trusty tractor and zoomed over the grass to meet them. He span around and then came to a screeching stop. Frightened chickens flew everywhere, and the sheep were so scared they tried to run away.

Farmer Riley was very cross. He shouted at Sonny and ordered him out of the field. "Sorry!" cried Sonny, and raced off.

Tony watched as Sonny rocketed down the track at top speed. "That car is going far too fast," said Farmer Riley. "Something will happen to him soon that might make him see sense."

Farmer Riley and Tony moved from field to field, sharing out food for the animals. Tony could still hear Sonny in the distance, and before long the sound grew louder and closer. Sonny hurtled into view and tore down the dusty track.

Suddenly, a startled sheep leapt across the path, right in front of Sonny. The car flung itself to one side to avoid crashing, and nearly knocked Farmer Riley off his feet. "Help!" cried the farmer. "Help!" beeped the car, as he realised he was headed straight for the pond.

Tony the tractor chugged down to see if the farmer was alright. He was a little bit muddy, but unharmed and unhurt.

"I'm not sure you can say the same for Sonny," chuckled Tony. "He's certainly slowed down, though."

Poor Sonny looked very sorry for himself. He was good at zooming around on the roads, but he wasn't a good swimmer at all! The farm animals laughed as Tony winched the poor little car out of the pond.

"That seems to have dampened his spirits!" smiled Farmer Riley. "NOW will you slow down, Sonny?"

Over the Moon

Teddy Fred can't sleep. He knows that he should close his eyes and try his hardest, but there are too many things to think about. He has been busy all day, but he can't wait until tomorrow so that he can do even more fun things.

Fred gazes around the room and notices Sharman the spaceman looking out of the window. "Can't you sleep either?" he whispers, and tiptoes across to the windowsill.

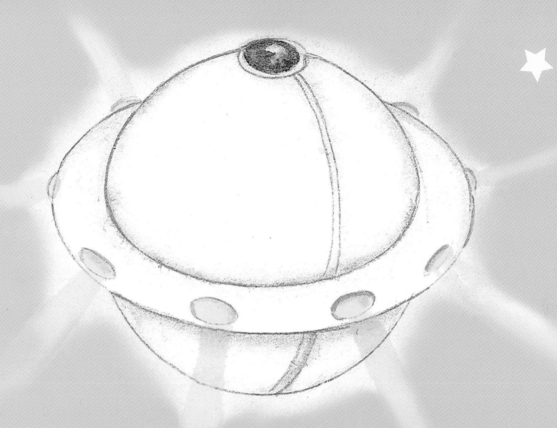

Sharman the spaceman doesn't like sleeping at night. He prefers to look out of the window and keep watch for flying saucers.

"Surely there is no such thing?" asks Teddy Fred.

Sharman can't believe what he is hearing. "Of course there is!" he exclaims, and then looks guiltily around the room. He is afraid he has woken the other toys, but they are all sleeping soundly.

Then they hear a steady buzzing noise that turns into a gentle "thrub–thrub–thrub." A yellow glow appears in the night sky. It is too big to be an aeroplane and too close to be a star. Teddy Fred gets very excited.

As the glow moves closer, Teddy Fred can see it more clearly. It is shaped like a ball and lit all over with strange lights that seem to hum and pulse.

"Follow me!" says Sharman,
and he opens the window a little
bit. It is a tiny gap, just big enough
for Sharman and then Teddy Fred
to climb through.

There is a loud hoot and
a screech that makes
Teddy Fred jump.

"Wha– ?" he exclaims,
wondering if he is going to be
zapped by an alien blaster.
Instead, he sees a frightened
owl staring at the strange
ball above them.

Suddenly, a shaft of bright light beams
down from the sky. The owl screeches
once more, and takes off silently to get
far away from this unusual flying
creature. Teddy Fred lifts his paw to
his eyes to shade them from the glare.

There is a whooshing noise and Teddy Fred feels awfully strange. He has pins and needles in his paws, and a twisty-turny feeling in his tummy. He looks down at his furry feet and realises that he is floating! Next to him, Sharman is smiling and waving at him from within the same shaft of light. They are being beamed up towards the spaceship!

Teddy Fred is so excited. This is one of the most fun things he could imagine! "Are we going to the Sun?" he asks Sharman.

"We can't do that," replies the spaceman. "But we can ask if they can fly us around the Moon. That's definitely worth seeing, and won't take long at all. Aliens do know how to travel super-fast!"

The aliens inside the spaceship are very friendly, but don't speak any language that Teddy Fred can understand. Instead of talking, Sharman draws a picture of the Moon. The aliens know exactly how to get there, and program their controls with the right directions.

Teddy Fred absolutely adores seeing the Moon. They fly right around it, four times, to get the best views. Sharman laughs. Teddy Fred is pressing his face so hard against the window that Sharman thinks he is going to fall out of the spaceship!

The Sun is only just beginning to rise when the aliens fly back to Earth. They press a button and their two passengers are beamed straight back into their beds. "Wow!" thinks Teddy Fred. "That was such an adventure. Now I'll NEVER want to go to sleep at night in case I miss something so exciting!"

Talent Show

The animals are getting together to put on a talent show. It is going to be a spectacular performance of some of the jungle's greatest acts.

"I'm going to be the world's tallest animal!" says Giraffe.

"That's not a talent, that's just the way you are!" says Zebra. "You have to think of something special to do."

"Being the world's tallest animal IS special," replies Giraffe. "But I admit, I do it all the time, so it isn't very exciting to watch in a show. I can yodel, though. That's what I'll do."

The frogs have formed an acrobatics team, and Zebra is planning to balance a ball on his nose. They all ask Tiger Cub what she is doing for the show.

Tiger Cub can't think of anything she's good at. She decides to find the other animals and see what they're going to do.

It's clear to see what the Hippo sisters will do. They are already practising their dance routine. They don't have any music, but Crocodile is snapping his jaws so they can keep in time.

Lion is telling jokes to make everyone laugh. Some of them are funny, but the animals are so scared of him that they even laugh at his rubbish jokes.

Tiger Cub wonders what Monkey is going to do.

"I'm a clown!" says Monkey. Hmm, he certainly is. He trips and falls when he tries to run, and gets dirt in his eyes when he juggles with mud balls. "Hee hee, that's really funny," snorts Warthog.

Tiger Cub listens to the elephants trumpeting a jolly marching tune. They are very loud. She covers her ears with her paws and wonders what other acts there are for her to try.

"What are you doing, Warthog?" she asks.

"I use mud to paint portraits," he snorts. "Sometimes you can even tell who they're supposed to be!"

Hmm, that doesn't sound all that good, thinks Tiger Cub.

Tiger Cub sits behind a tree and wonders what part she can play in the talent show. She can hear snapping and trumpeting, and she can see leaping and tumbling. She can even see snakes in the branches doing a loop the loop display that looks as if they have tied themselves in knots.

Some of these acts seem very good, and Tiger Cub can't think of anything she can do so well. On the other hand, some of them might need more practise, so she should be able to try hard and be just as good.

But WHAT can she do that no-one else is doing already?

Then Tiger Cub has a flash of inspiration.

"I know what I can do for the show!" she roars,
and jumps to her feet.

The other animals gather around.
"Well," asks Giraffe, "what hidden talents do you
have? Are you going to be the star of the show?"

"Well, funny you should say that, Giraffe – but in a
kind of way, I am," explains Tiger Cub. "I have realised
that one vital thing is missing, and it's something
I'm good at. I am going to be the judge of the show,
and decide who is the very best act of all! And nobody
will dare to disagree with me – RARRRRR!" she roars,
in her baby tiger voice.

The other animals all laugh, and agree that a good
judge is just the thing they need.

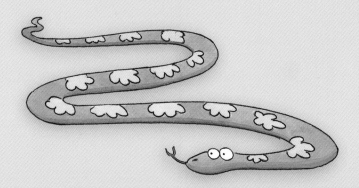

King for a Day

Jack was very excited. He had won first prize in a competition. His prize was to be the King for a whole day!

Jack was a little bit nervous when he met the real King.

"Don't worry, my boy," said the King. "I have written you a full set of instructions, and my servant Lizzie here will help you if you need her."

With that, the King handed over his robes and his crown, and bounded off to have fun for the day.

"Oh – " he called, as he left the room. "Just one warning – it does get a bit boring!"

Jack was quite shocked, but he sat on the throne and read through the instructions.

Jack's list contained a whole lot of jobs that needed to be done. Some of them did look a bit boring – and some of them looked REEEEEALLY boring. Poor Jack!

Lizzie came over to look through the list. She pointed out some fun things that they could do. "Look," she said. "Counting the royal treasure is okay, and eating a royal banquet is excellent.

And you can have an afternoon nap in the royal four-poster bed. Then you can ride all of the King's horses, if you want?"

Jack pointed to the top item on the list. He had a meeting with Wizard Potemkin. "That must be fun?" he asked. "I've never met a real wizard!"

Lizzie grimaced. She explained that Wizard Potemkin was the biggest moaner in all the land, and that the King hated meeting with him.

Jack didn't like the sound of that. Maybe he could do the King a favour, and get rid of the Wizard once and for all? He asked Lizzie if she would help him hatch a plan.

When the wizard walked into the throne room, he was surprised to see a young boy sitting in the King's place. He marched straight up to Jack and started his moaning. He was so rude he didn't even ask Jack's name.

Jack listened to him for five minutes and then held up his hand. "By the power vested in me, for today only, as a one-chance special offer, may I make a suggestion?"

Jack told the wizard that he would let him take charge for an hour, as long as the wizard promised faithfully to do all of the royal tasks on Jack's list.

The wizard liked the sound of that! Just imagine – him as the ruler for a while! He rubbed his hands together and agreed to the deal.

"Do you definitely promise?" checked Jack. "Do you give me your word as a Grade 1 wizard that you will do every single job on this list?"

The wizard swore on his wizarding certificate. Jack handed over the robes and went to stand by the door with Lizzie. First of all, the wizard called for the royal treasure to count. He waved his wand so that all the money flew into piles and counted itself. Easy!

Then he looked at the second task. His smile turned to a frown and he stood up in a rage. "Nooooooo!" he shouted, and wisps of blue smoke came out of his ears.

At that moment, the King popped back in to see how Jack was doing. He was just in time to see Wizard Potemkin march out in a total rage. "Whatever is going on?" asked the King.

Jack couldn't stop grinning as he explained to the King. When he showed the list to him, the King chuckled. "Banish all Wizards lower than Grade 2 level!" he laughed. "That is a very clever plan, my lad. You are doing such a good job at this King business, I'll leave you to it. Don't eat all of my royal cake, though!"

An Amazing Day

Grandpa Mike is a pilot. He flies all sorts of aeroplanes, big and small. Some of them are little private jets that take rich people to important meetings. Some of the planes are huge liners that carry hundreds of people to their holiday destinations.

Grandpa Mike works at a very busy airport. He wears a smart uniform with gold braid on the shoulders and sleeves. His grandchildren, Daisy and Danny, love to see him dressed so smartly. If they ask nicely, he lets them try on his pilot's hat. It is way too big and covers their eyes. "That wouldn't be much good for flying a plane," he laughs, and ruffles their hair.

Today, Daisy and Danny are at the airport with Grandpa Mike. They would happily spend hours watching the planes land and take off. They use their binoculars to spot the jets coming in from far away, and pretend they are guiding them in to the runway, just like an air traffic controller.

"Look, Grandpa," cries Daisy. "There's a helicopter coming! It's a bright red one! I wonder if it will land here?"

Sure enough, the helicopter hovers over one of the airstrips and gently comes down to land. Grandpa Mike's walkie talkie crackles and buzzes, and he listens to the lady talking to him.

"Hmm, we have a small problem," says Grandpa. "That chopper needs to take its cargo to a special delivery address, but the pilot has finished his flying hours. He's not allowed to fly again until he has had some sleep. They want me to finish the job. Will you come with me?"

"Can we really come?" shriek Danny and Daisy. "We've never been in a helicopter!"

Grandpa Mike clears it with his airline to make sure he can carry two young, excited passengers. He gathers up the paperwork and leads them through the airport.

They walk outside to make their way to the helicopter. It is so noisy out here! Daisy covers her ears to protect them from the scream of engines. Danny grabs his Grandpa as a plane comes in to land nearby and makes him jump.

Together, they run to the helicopter and Grandpa helps them climb in and buckle up. The pilot is coming with them to get back home, but he will try to sleep on the journey.

As the helicopter blades begin to whirr and buzz, Danny claps his hands excitedly. The chopper lifts gracefully into the air and then moves forward. Daisy can't stop smiling. It is such an amazing feeling!

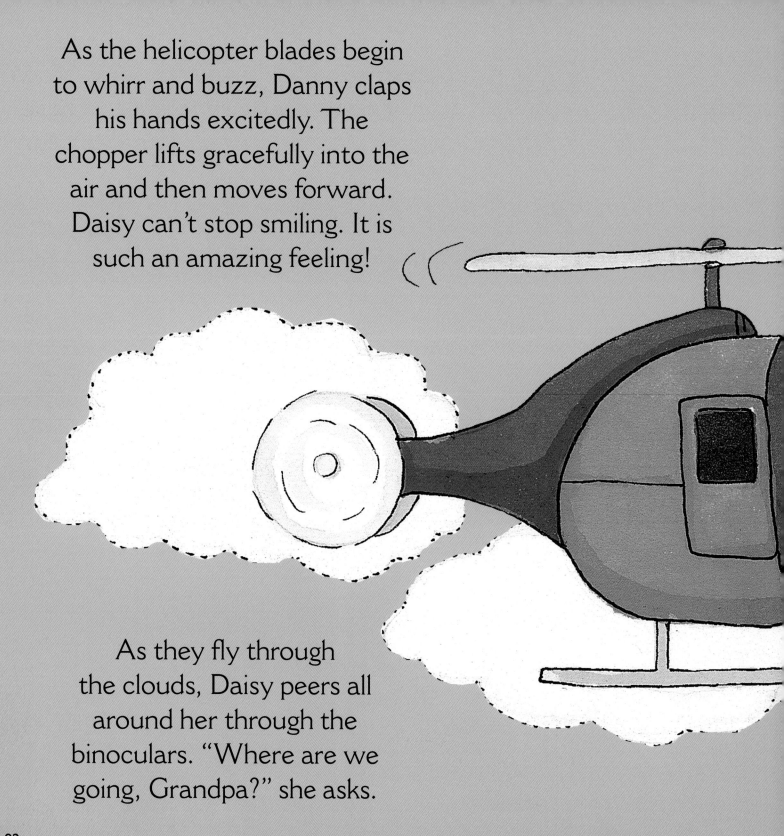

As they fly through the clouds, Daisy peers all around her through the binoculars. "Where are we going, Grandpa?" she asks.

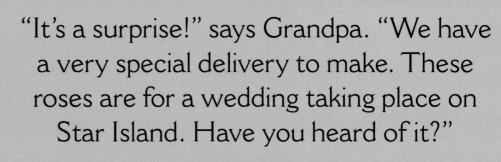

"It's a surprise!" says Grandpa. "We have a very special delivery to make. These roses are for a wedding taking place on Star Island. Have you heard of it?"

Daisy and Danny look at each other. They certainly have heard of it – but surely it can't be true…?

Daisy hands the binoculars to Danny and whispers, "I think we're nearly there. Look – down below!"

Grandpa nods. "Yes, this is it. The pilot can guide us down now as he's landed here many times before. Are you ready for this?"

The helicopter drops lower and lower and then gently comes to rest in a clearing. When the rotors have stopped whirring, they all jump out and unload armfuls of roses. Then their favourite pop singer appears in a gleaming white suit.
It is Justin Starr!

"Thank you so much for these, you're just in time," he says. "Will you be stopping for the wedding and a slice of cake?"

Daisy can't decide what's best: flying in a helicopter, going to Justin Starr's wedding, or having such an amazing Grandpa. "All three!" laughs Danny, and hugs Grandpa Mike tightly.

Helpful Heathcliff

Heathcliff is a dragon. He isn't a scary dragon, but people think that he is. He lives alone in Wuthering Woods, and only the bravest people go there. There are even signs saying BEWARE OF THE DRAGON pinned to the trees.

Every time new people visit the woods, Heathcliff tries to be friendly. But the sight of a dragon is enough to scare them away.

"Excuse me, you have dropped your lunch," says Heathcliff – but the picnickers run and leave it.

"I'm sorry, are these your books?" he asks – but the parents hurry their children back to the car.
Poor Heathcliff. He is only trying to be helpful.

One day in the summer, Heathcliff is walking through the trees, listening to the birds chirping and the insects buzzing. They aren't afraid of him, so he doesn't understand why creatures as large and powerful as humans are frightened.

"They don't understand," explains his friend Squirrel. "They have all sorts of stories about how scary dragons are. They think you are going to eat them, or at least breathe fire all over them!"

Heathcliff scuffs through the grass and wonders what to do. As if he isn't feeling miserable enough already, it begins to rain. Huge drops plop onto his snout and trickle off his wings. He is officially a down-in-the dumps dragon.

As Heathcliff tries to shelter beneath a tree,
he hears voices.

"This confounded rain!" says a grown-up voice.
"How are we supposed to light a barbecue in this
weather? I say we just pack up and go home."

"Aw, pleeeeeease Dad, can we stay? I'll try to find
some dry twigs under the trees."

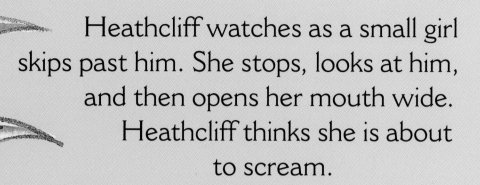

Heathcliff watches as a small girl skips past him. She stops, looks at him, and then opens her mouth wide. Heathcliff thinks she is about to scream.

Instead, she takes a step closer. "Are you a dragon?" she says. "Like, a real one, that breathes fire and everything?"

Heathcliff smiles and puffs out a few flames. The little girl looks delighted. "Stay here!" she says. "Please?"

The girl skips back to her family and announces that she wants to play hide and seek. "Please can we?" she begs. "Just for a while, to see if it stops raining? I'll be the seeker and count to 100. Go!" she shouts, and starts counting. "One…two…three…"

When the others have run off, she fetches Heathcliff from his hiding place.

"Would you be a very kind dragon and breathe fire onto our barbecue?" she asks.

Heathcliff is more than happy to help. He gently puffs hot air over the coals to make sure they are dry, and then breathes flames onto them until they catch fire. The little girl hugs him and says thank you. Then she carries on counting.

"Ninety nine…a hundred!" she shouts loudly. "Coming, ready or not!"

As Susie finds her family in their hiding places, she tells each of them what she has seen. Of course, none of them believe her.

"It's true," she pleads. "Look, he made our barbecue come alight!"

Her parents look at each other and raise their eyebrows. They say nothing but start to cook their food. The sausages and burgers smell delicious, and Heathcliff hides nearby to breathe in the lovely smells. Then he notices the little girl throwing sausages in his direction when the others aren't looking.

"My goodness, Susie," says her mum. "How many sausages have you eaten? It's a good job we did get this barbecue going – you were obviously hungry!"

Heathcliff feels much happier now. He's glad he could help – and he does love sausages!

Knock Knock

It is night time in the toy room, and all of the toys want to play. Teddy asks if they can have a game of football. "I'm wearing my football kit!" he says, "so I want to play!"

The others agree that he is dressed in the right outfit, so they find a football and start to kick it around. But none of them are very good, and they soon get bored.

"Let's do races!" says Mega Mouse. But the others know that he always wins, so it isn't any fun. They don't have wheels and a wind-up key like he does.

"I know," says Happy Clown. "There's a new toy over there. Shall I get that for us to play with?"

The other toys haven't noticed the box in the corner. Happy Clown pushes it into the middle of the room.

The toys all crowd around the box excitedly.
Happy Clown steps to the front and grins.

"I love this toy!" he says. "I hope you do, too!"
He presses the button on the front.

The toys all shriek and tumble backwards in
alarm as a strange person on a giant spring
leaps out at them.

"Waaaah!" cries Teddy.
"What is it? I don't like it!"

Mega Mouse turns on his wheels and zooms
into a corner to hide. The toy in the box
stands there wobbling on his spring and
waving his arms at them. His smile has
turned to a sad face and he has a tear
in his eye.

Happy Clown is sad, too. He wants his friends to welcome the new toy, not be afraid of it.

"This is Jack," says Happy Clown. "It's his job to spring out of his box and make you jump."

"Well, I don't like it," says Teddy. "Toys are supposed to make you happy, not scared. Make it go away!"

Happy Clown pushes Jack back into the box and fastens the lid closed. Poor Jack squats inside and wonders what to do. He doesn't want people to leave him shut away the whole time. He wipes his tears and tries to think of a solution to the problem.

Jack hears a tiny knock and a squeak coming from outside his box. It is Mega Mouse.

"Excuse me, Mr Jack, but we would like to see you again. Could you come out more quietly this time, please?"

Jack hears a fumbling noise and then his button is pressed. BOING! He leaps out of the box.

The other toys are standing quite a distance away, so they aren't so scared this time. At least they were expecting him!

Jack explains that
it is impossible for
him to come
out quietly.
"It's just the way
I'm made," he says
sadly. "My spring is
so springy that
I have to bounce
right out!"

They all agree that Jack shouldn't have to change just to please them.

"We need to find a way to play together properly," says Teddy. Happy Clown thinks he has a plan.

Now, whenever Jack is going to come out to play, he has a special code. He taps on the inside of his box and shouts, "Knock, knock!"

When the others hear him, they reply, "Who's there?" and he must call out, "Jack!"

"Jack who?" they shriek, and press the button on his box.

Then Jack jumps out and cries, "Jack in the box!" and it makes them all laugh. Now that they know he is coming, his bouncing and springing doesn't make them jump any more!

It's a Record

Beefy is a big, yellow digger. In fact, he's more than big. He's enormous. He thunders around the building site on his giant caterpillar tracks, boasting about how great he is.

"I can dig bigger holes than any of YOU," he sneers. "And I can carry more earth, and I can cover rougher ground, and I can lift my bucket way higher than you can even see!"

Benjy is not such a big digger. He is quite small, and red, but very useful to have around. He is also much nicer and nowhere near such a bore.

"What can I do to help today?" he asks.

Beefy is digging in the schoolyard when he hears the crunch of metal against metal. His blades have touched something buried in the ground.

"I know what that is!" hollers Beefy, as Benjy trundles over to take a closer look. "It's a…it's a…what is it?"

Benjy doesn't know what it is either, but his scoop is small enough to dig beneath the metal object and carefully prise it out of the earth. He slowly turns to one side and deposits it on the ground.

Bert, the builder in charge, and Mrs Collins, the head teacher of the school, peer at the object. "Do you think it could be…? Well, it certainly looks like… Oh, I do hope it is!"

Beefy is getting twitchy now. He hates not knowing what is going on. "Oh, now it's out of the ground, I know exactly what it is," he gloats. "It's a…it's a blue thing!" he declares proudly.

Benjy looks quizzically at Beefy. "Oh, really?" he asks. "And what kind of a blue thing, exactly? Sometimes, Beefy, you should learn to keep quiet. Just watch and listen and don't pretend to know everything."

Beefy isn't happy to be spoken to like that. But his nosiness gets the better of him, and instead of telling Benjy off, he listens to the people talking.

Mrs Collins explains to the children that the blue thing is a time capsule – a kind of treasure chest full of things  from long ago. They will open it and see what's inside, but they must be very careful in case the things are fragile and precious.

Benjy is excited and trundles closer to look. Beefy wants to look, too, but Bert holds up his hand sternly. "Now then, Beefy, you must stay back. I don't want your massive tracks crushing anything of value."

Beefy reverses a little way, but he can't see what is going on. He edges closer and closer.

"Well, I never!" exclaims Mrs Collins. "An old gramophone! It must be a hundred years old!"

The children have never heard of a gramophone. Neither has Beefy. He creeps closer to the group again to listen.

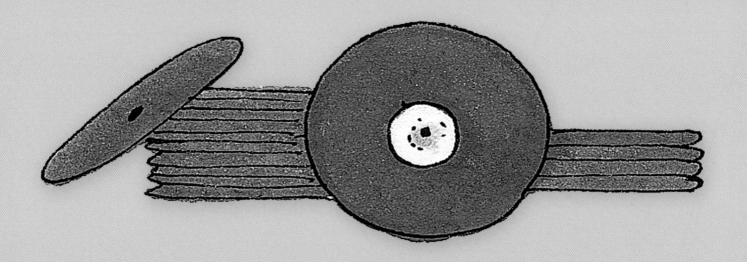

"A gramophone is a very old record player," explains Mrs Collins. "Records are like an old-fashioned version of CDs. They go round and round and the recorded music comes out of this trumpet-shaped piece on top."

Beefy is excited, and moves a little closer. He sends a shower of earth tumbling back down into the hole.

"Beefy!" says Bert. "I'm sorry, but you're just too big to be this close! Go back and wait outside the schoolyard!"

Poor Beefy! Now he is too far away to see what else is in the chest. He has to listen to the squeals and yells from the children as they uncover more surprises.

Benjy is happy to get up close and watch the treasure as it is pulled out of the chest. There are old clothes, toys and lots of old-fashioned black and white photographs. The class carefully takes them all inside to use in a school project.

Luckily, the gramophone still works. Bert cleans it and winds it up, and then places a record on top. The sound is very scratchy, but a tune comes out. Benjy can hear it playing from his parking spot outside. At least he isn't missing out on all the fun!